Hello, Family Members,

Learning to read is one of the most important accomplishments of early childhood. **Hello Reader!** books are designed to help children become skilled readers who like to read. Beginning readers learn to read by remembering frequently used words like "the," "is," and "and"; by using phonics skills to decode new words; and by interpreting picture and text clues. These books provide both the stories children enjoy and the structure they need to read fluently and independently. Here are suggestions for helping your child *before*, *during*, and *after* reading:

Before

- Look at the cover and pictures and have your child predict what the story is about.
- Read the story to your child.
- Encourage your child to chime in with familiar words and phrases.
- Echo read with your child by reading a line first and having your child read it after you do.

During

- Have your child think about a word he or she does not recognize right away. Provide hints such as "Let's see if we know the sounds" and "Have we read other words like this one?"
- Encourage your child to use phonics skills to sound out new words.
- Provide the word for your child when more assistance is needed so that he or she does not struggle and the experience of reading with you is a positive one.
- Encourage your child to have fun by reading with a lot of expression . . . like an actor!

After

- Have your child keep lists of interesting and favorite words.
- Encourage your child to read the books over and over again. Have him or her read to brothers, sisters, grandparents, and even teddy bears. Repeated readings develop confidence in young readers.
- Talk about the stories. Ask and answer questions. Share ideas about the funniest and most interesting characters and events in the stories.

I do hope that you and your child enjoy this book.

—Francie Alexander
Reading Specialist,
Scholastic's Learning Ventures

To Beatrice de Regniers,
whom I will never forget.
—E.M.

To our granddaughters, JiJi and Mei Lu,
whom we love to reward.
—E.R. & D.B.

ISBN 0-590-92921-6

Text copyright © 2001 by Eva Moore.
Illustrations copyright © 2001 by Don Bolognese.
All rights reserved. Published by Scholastic Inc.
SCHOLASTIC, HELLO READER, CARTWHEEL BOOKS and associated logos are
trademarks and/or registered trademarks of Scholastic Inc.

Library of Congress Cataloging-in-Publication Data

Moore, Eva.
    Good children get rewards / by Eva Moore ; illustrated by Don Bolognese/Elaine
Raphael.
        p.   cm.— (Hello reader! Level 4)
    "Cartwheel Books."
    Summary: As a brother and sister follow the directions in a rebus letter they
discover in their father's shop, they are led to help people in various places throughout
eighteenth-century Williamsburg.
    ISBN 0-590-92921-6 (pbk.)
    1.Rebuses. [1. Conduct of life—Fiction. 2. Brothers and sisters—Fiction. 3.
Williamsburg (Va.)—History—Colonial period, ca. 1600-1775—Fiction. 4. Rebuses.]
I. Bolognese, Don, ill.   II. Raphael, Elaine, ill.   III. Title.   IV. Series.
PZ7.M7835 Go   2000
[E] — dc21   99-046435

10 9 8 7 6 5 4 3   01 02 03 04 05

Printed in the U.S.A.
First printing, February 2001

24

Good Children Get Rewards

A Story of Williamsburg in Colonial Times

by Eva Moore
Illustrated by Don Bolognese
and Elaine Raphael

Hello Reader! — Level 4

Colonial Williamsburg Foundation

Williamsburg, Virginia

SCHOLASTIC INC.

New York　　Toronto　　London　　Auckland　　Sydney
Mexico City　　New Delhi　　Hong Kong

Ann and Tom's father had a shop in
the town of Williamsburg, Virginia.
He made and sold tables and chairs and
chests and desks.

One morning, Ann and Tom were alone in their father's shop. Tom was playing with the drawers of a desk.

"Look, Ann. This drawer has a secret place in the back," he said. "And there's something in it!"

Tom unrolled the paper.

"It has writing and pictures," he said.

"It's a rebus!" said Ann.

"I think it is a message for us."

To the  who find this :

The shines on who do

good deeds. Do you the small

behind this ?

good and carry the to

the shop where they make for .

Go now and quick. You will get a

n + SUR + PURR + 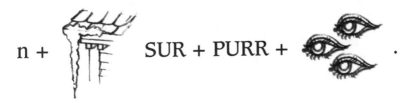 .

"Do you think Father left us this rebus?" Ann asked.

"I don't know," Tom said.

"I know where the Shoemaker's Shop is," said Ann. "It's on Duke of Gloucester Street."

"Let's go," Tom said. "I wonder what kind of surprise we'll find."

"Hello, children," the shoemaker said.
"Thank you for bringing my table."

Tom and Ann waited for their surprise.
But instead, the shoemaker handed them a
pair of boots.

"As long as you are here, would you take
these over to the Prentis Store? They are for
Mr. Prentis."

Tom and Ann walked around the corner
and up the street to the Prentis Store.

The storekeeper's wife was there.

"Here are your husband's boots, Mrs. Prentis," said Ann. "Do you have a surprise for us?"

Mrs. Prentis looked puzzled. "A surprise? No, I dare say I do not. But good children are sure to get rewards. As long as you are here, would you take this lantern to the blacksmith? Our shipment of goods from England just arrived, and he has been waiting for a new lantern."

The blacksmith took the lantern and handed them a hoe.

"You came at the right time. Be good children, will you, and take this hoe to the Powells' house? I have just finished mending it."

What could Tom and Ann do? They carried the hoe across the street and around the corner and down another street. It was a long way to the Powells' house.

Rose, the kitchen gardener, was outside. She was glad to have the hoe again. "What good children you are!" she said. "It will be so much easier to weed now." Tom and Ann turned to go.

"Wait!" said Rose. "As long as you are here, would you take these herbs to the milliner for Mrs. Powell?"

The milliner's shop was full of all kinds of goods for sale—ribbons and lace, gloves and fans, buttons and babies' caps.

The milliner was sewing a ribbon onto a small, padded cap.

"Oh," said the milliner, "how good you are to bring these herbs. I will dry them to make tea."

She finished her sewing.

"Now run along," she said, "and take this pudding cap to the miller's wife. It is for her new baby boy."

Ann and Tom took
the cap to the miller's wife.
She gave them a sack of
cornmeal to take to the cooper...

and he gave them a water bucket.

"I must finish this barrel by dinnertime," he said. "Would you good children take this bucket to the harnessmaker for me? I told him he would have it today."

Tom and Ann wondered if they would ever find the surprise that the rebus promised. They were getting tired from walking all over town.

Suddenly, they heard shouts.

"Fire! Fire!"

A woman ran past Tom and Ann.

"Hurry, children!" she called. "We need you for the bucket brigade!"

The town's fire engine had been pulled up in front of a tavern. People formed two lines from the well to the fire engine.

Tom drew a bucket of water from the well and passed it to Ann. Ann passed it to the next person in line, who handed it down to the next person. More buckets went down the line in the same way.

The water was poured into the fire engine and pumped out the long pipe onto the flames.

Everyone was glad when the fire was out.

Ann saw the harnessmaker. "We were bringing you this bucket from the cooper," she told him, "but we ran into the fire."

"We used your bucket in the bucket brigade!" Tom said.

The harnessmaker smiled.

"You are good children indeed," he said.
"You must be tired after all that work.
Come, let me give you
a ride home."

Ann and Tom waved to everyone as they
rode down Duke of Gloucester Street.

At home, they ran inside and found their father waiting for them.

"Where have you two been all morning?" he asked. "Didn't you want your surprise?"

"Papa," Ann said. "I *knew* you wrote the rebus! You will never guess. We've been all over town doing errands for people. It was a day full of surprises."

"I am proud to have children who help their neighbors," their father said. "Good children get rewards."

Ann's reward was a beautiful doll.

"I carved the head myself," her father said. "Your mother sewed the clothes."

Tom got a kite with a long tail.

"Let's take it out and fly it now," said Tom.

"Not so fast," their father said. "It's almost time for dinner. I think your mother has made gingerbread cakes for dessert."

The gingerbread cakes were good.
At last, Ann and Tom got their rewards.

A note about this story

This story takes place a long time ago, about the year 1773. It is not a true story. Tom and Ann and their parents are made-up characters, but they are like people who lived in those days. And the town in the story is real. The streets, the shops, the clothes, and even the fire engine are true to life.

Today, Williamsburg, Virginia, is a big city. But many of the buildings from the 1770s are still there in a special town-within-the-city called Colonial Williamsburg. People from all over the world visit the town to see how people lived more than 200 years ago, before there were electric lights, cars, trains, airplanes, televisions, movies, computers, and lots of other things we have today.

Life was very different then, but some things are still the same. Mothers and fathers loved their children and took good care of them. Children were expected to help

ad time to p
illiamsburg, you
re, the blacksmith's
shop, and other places in
see some people dressed
in the story. You might even
clothes like those Ann and Tom
g and take part in a bucket
to put out a fire.

en if you don't have the chance to go
Colonial Williamsburg, you can visit it
every time you open this book and look at
the pictures.

figure out the rebus
...n and Tom?

...o the <u>children</u> who find this <u>note</u>:

The <u>sun</u> shines on <u>children</u> who do

good deeds. Do you <u>see</u> the small <u>table</u>

behind this <u>desk</u>?

<u>Be</u> good <u>dears</u> and carry the <u>table</u> to

the shop where they make <u>boots</u> for <u>men</u>.

Go now and <u>be</u> quick. You will get a

<u>nice</u> <u>surprise</u>.

**Did you figure out the rebus
with Ann and Tom?**

To the <u>children</u> who find this <u>note</u>:

The <u>sun</u> shines on <u>children</u> who do

good deeds. Do you <u>see</u> the small <u>table</u>

behind this <u>desk</u>?

<u>Be</u> good <u>dears</u> and carry the <u>table</u> to

the shop where they make <u>boots</u> for <u>men</u>.

Go now and <u>be</u> quick. You will get a

<u>nice</u> <u>surprise</u>.

out at home, but they still had time to play.

If you go to Colonial Williamsburg, you will see the Prentis Store, the blacksmith's shop, the milliner's shop, and other places in the story. You will see some people dressed like the people in the story. You might even get to try on clothes like those Ann and Tom are wearing and take part in a bucket brigade to put out a fire.

Even if you don't have the chance to go to Colonial Williamsburg, you can visit it every time you open this book and look at the pictures.